My Teacher is an

ELF

D1314049

This book is dedicated to our kids,
Grayson and Ella, who always keep us on
our toes and make every day magical.

This is also dedicated to Mrs. Acker's
students who still wonder to this day if she
is an elf.

The Wonder Who Crew: Book 2
Copyright © 2018 Joey and Melanie Acker
All rights reserved.
ISBN: 0692967419
ISBN-13: 978-0692967416

My Teacher is an Elf

By Joey and Melanie Acker

There's something very special
about my teacher, Ms. Holly.

She is always cheerful and says that everything is magical...

even homework...

When we walk down the hall in a very quiet line, I always hear a jingle when she walks.

jingle jingle jingle

Maybe she is hiding bells.

Ms. Holly loves to sing songs. We sing in the morning, during math, and when we clean up.

Isn't that something all elves do?

Ms. Holly wears pointy shoes to school every day. How does she even get her toes in there?

Elves are great at making gifts.

Ms. Holly is also very crafty.

Every time I see elves, they are drinking
hot cocoa to get their day started.

Ms. Holly always has a big cup of
something warm in the morning.

She keeps a list of who is being naughty and nice in our class. Maybe she is helping Santa.

Elves' favorite things to eat are cookies and chocolate. Ms. Holly eats a lot of chocolate when she is teaching.

Ms. Holly always wears her hair down at school.
I wonder what she is hiding under there.

Seeing kids' happiness brings joy
to elves.

Ms. Holly says we make her
happy every day.

Whether she is an elf or not, I am
glad she is our teacher.

We hope you enjoyed our "story"!

Joey and Melanie both began their careers working together in daycares and then became school teachers. They still work in education today and are married with two wonderful children, Grayson and Ella.